My Favorite Dogs

LABRADOR RETRIEVER

Jinny Johnson

A+
Smart Apple Media

Published by Smart Apple Media
P.O. Box 1329
Mankato, MN 56002

Printed in the United States of America,
at Corporate Graphics in North Mankato, Minnesota.

Designed by Hel James
Edited by Mary-Jane Wilkins

Library of Congress Cataloging-in-Publication Data

Johnson, Jinny, 1949-
  Labrador retriever / by Jinny Johnson.
     p. cm. -- (My favorite dog)
  Includes index.
  Summary: "Describes the care, training, and rearing of the Labrador retriever.
Also explains the Labrador retriever's unique characteristics
and history"--Provided by publisher.
  ISBN 978-1-59920-844-2 (hardcover, library bound)
  1. Labrador retriever--Juvenile literature. I. Title.
  SF429.L3J614 2013
  636.752'7--dc23
                        2012012145

Photo acknowledgements
t = top, b = bottom
page 1 Tina Rencelj/Shutterstock; 3 c.byatt-norman/Shutterstock; 4 Gorilla/
Shutterstock; 5 Pawel Cebo/Shutterstock; 6 iStockphoto/Thinkstock; 7 Gerald
Marella/Shutterstock; 8-9 Erik Lam/Shutterstock; 10-11 Teresa Kasprzycka/
Shutterstock; 12 iStockphoto/Thinkstock; 13t Ryan McVay/Thinkstock,
b ARENA Creative/Shutterstock; 14 iStockphoto/Thinkstock; 15 karam Miri/
Shutterstock; 16-17 Vlad Ageshin/Shutterstock; 18 Hemera/Thinkstock;
19 Huntstock/Thinkstock; 20 Tatiana Gass/Shutterstock;
21 aspen rock Shutterstock; 23 Gorilla/Shutterstock
Cover Eric Isselée/Shutterstock

DAD0504
042012
9 8 7 6 5 4 3 2 1

Contents

I'm a Labrador Retriever!

I'm a big softie. I'm lovable, brave, and loyal and I'll do anything for my family. I love to help and I love to please. I'm good with children, too.

What I Need

I like to work hard and play hard, and I need a good walk every day. I'm happy running alongside when my owner goes for a run or a bike ride. I enjoy playing games and fetching sticks and balls, too.

I love being part of the family and
don't like being left alone for long.

The Labrador Retriever

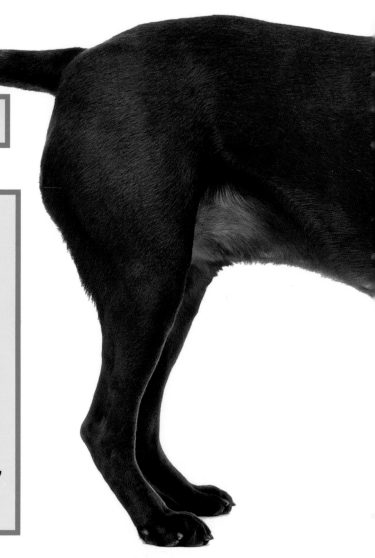

Thick, tapering tail

Height:
21½–24½ inches
(54½–62 cm)

Weight:
55–80 pounds
(25–36 kg)

Color: yellow, black,
or chocolate brown

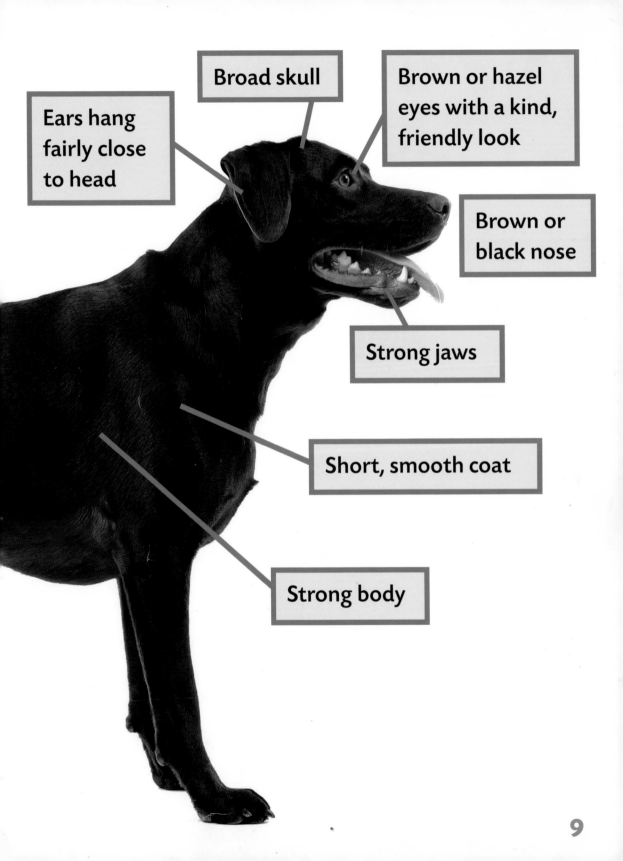

Broad skull

Brown or hazel eyes with a kind, friendly look

Ears hang fairly close to head

Brown or black nose

Strong jaws

Short, smooth coat

Strong body

All About Labradors

Labradors are from Newfoundland, Canada. They used to work with fishermen, helping to pull in nets and grab fish that tried to escape.

Some Labradors worked as sporting dogs, fetching catches for hunters.

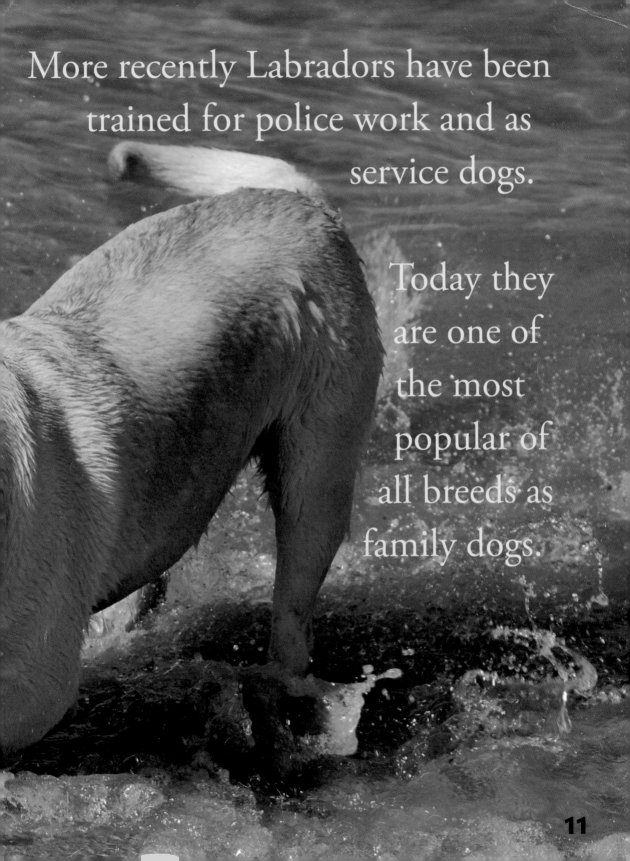

More recently Labradors have been trained for police work and as service dogs.

Today they are one of the most popular of all breeds as family dogs.

Growing Up

Labrador puppies are very cute, but they grow into big dogs. Like all pups, Labradors should stay with mom for about eight weeks before going to a new home.

A Labrador misses her mom when she first goes to her new home.

Be extra kind
and gentle with
your little pup
and she will
soon learn
to love her
human family.

Training Your Dog

Labradors are easy to train, as they are willing to do tasks for their owners and like to please.

It is important to train your Labrador when she's young and to show her that you are her pack leader.

Labradors can be trained to do important work, such as sniffing out forbidden items at airports.

Water Dogs

Labradors love water and are always ready for a swim. The dog uses its thick tail to steer itself in water.

Webbing between the dog's toes helps it doggy paddle fast.

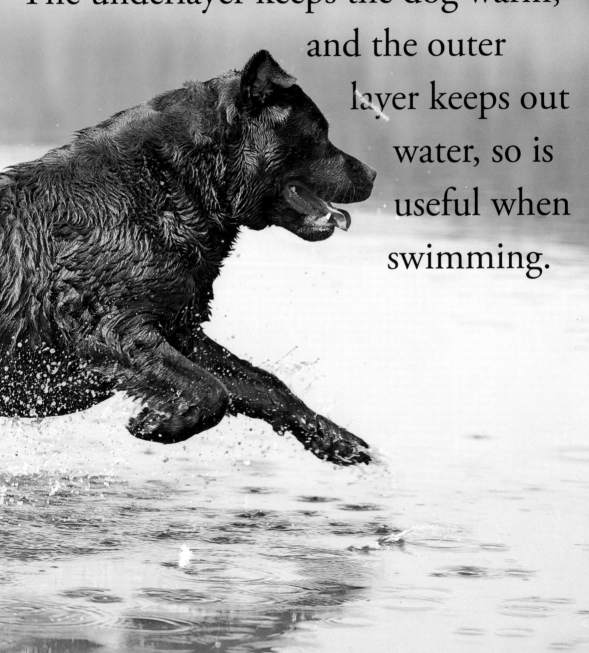

A Labrador has a double coat.
The underlayer keeps the dog warm,
and the outer
layer keeps out
water, so is
useful when
swimming.

Working Dogs

Today, Labradors are very popular service dogs, helping people who are blind or have other disabilities.

These dogs are confident, trustworthy, and hard working.

Not every pup is right for this work. Teaching a service dog the skills it

needs takes between 18 months and two years.

Your Healthy Dog

Your Labrador needs a good brush once a week to keep her coat in good condition. Only bathe her when she

is really dirty. Check her teeth and make sure she gets used to you brushing them when she's a pup.

Have your pup checked before buying to make sure she will not have bone

or joint problems. Labradors can have eye problems too.

Don't give your pup too much food; these dogs can easily become fat.

Caring for Your Dog

You and your family must think very carefully before buying a Labrador retriever. Remember, she may live as long as 11 years.

Every day your dog must have food, water, and exercise, as well as lots of love and care. She will need to go to the vet for checks and vaccinations. When you and your family go out or away on vacation, she will have to be looked after.

Useful Words

breed
A particular type of dog.

service dog
A dog that is specially trained to help people with disabilities or illnesses.

vaccinations
Injections given by the vet to protect your dog against certain illnesses.

Index